A POCKET FULL OF FLASH

An Anthology for the Curious

Heather Hawk

Table of Contents

Dedication..7

Editor's Note..11

1 Nanisms...13

    The Twins...13

    RV Life in a Van...13

    Unnamed...13

    Potentially a First Date............................14

    Reincarnation..14

    Treasured..15

    Twins..15

2 50 Word Shorts...17

    Identity Crisis...17

    Birth and Fate..17

    The Last Thread.......................................18

    Hoarding...18

    Waiting for the Melt................................19

    A Government Drone Surveilling a
Global Movement......................................19

    Imagine..20

    Inevitable...20

    Self-Portrait..21

    Disparity of Thanksgiving Festivities.....21

    The Sleep...22

    Night Jogging...22

Midnight Snack..22

Double Image..23

Cloud – Circa 1980..23

Sentiment...24

All Dressed Up and Nowhere to Go......................24

1970s Alternate Universe.....................................24

Pure Model for Social Services............................25

In Defense of Nature..25

3 100 Word Epiphanies......................................27

Poor Jacob..27

The Glass Menagerie..28

Dreaming of a Dinosaur.......................................29

A Last Meal Nightmare...29

Stasis..30

"Wingmans" Diverted Flight Path........................31

One Cutting Day in a Life.....................................32

Boredom...33

Nine Lives Are Not Just For Cats.........................33

Deep Dive Bar..34

Bondage – (a play date).......................................35

Cloud - circa 1994..36

Riding on Silk...37

The Crush...38

Eavesdropping-Who's Really the
Nosey Neighbor?..39

Decisions..40

The Embrace of Pillows..40

The Case for Restricting AI Use to Grown-Ups......41

Secrets on the Lips...42

Betrayal From a Dog's View....................................43

4 Flash Fiction...*45*

Dumbfounded..45

In Love with Whom? (Oreocereus celsianus)..........46

Clay Will Bind Us Together....................................47

House Hunting...49

Viewpoint Encased By Windows.............................51

The Haunt...53

The Mad Hatter Chef...58

The End of the World at a Kung Fu Temple............65

A New Year's Forecast..69

Annie's Eyes..77

The End of Nancy Drew..83

A Woof in the Dark..86

What A Boy Needs..88

Meet our Storytellers...*93*

Works by Author...*97*

Dedication

To all new and aspiring writers.

Dreams last five minutes.
Yet we can live a lifetime in one night.
Heather Hawk

Editor's Note

The sections on Nanisms, 50 Word Shorts, and 100 Word Epiphanies were written by Heather Hawk.

For the 50 and 100 word stories I enjoyed using word prompts from my writing groups. The prompt is repeated throughout a story and used in different contexts. After the title on several of the stories, in italics, the authors share the inspiration that prompted their writings.

In the Flash Fiction section, we are pleased to introduce newer and returning authors. The stories draw on fantasy, romantasy, science fiction, and ask for your imagination to soar.

1 Nanisms

Heather Hawk

The Twins

Our married friends ask, "Who do you *think* we would be if we each were the opposite sex?"

Joe and I reply in unison, "Why, you would be each other."

RV Life in a Van

"Move over. A narrow aisle makes it hard to get dressed. Do you realize you are in the way?"

"Yes love. That's the idea."

Unnamed

"Doc, I feel unwell."

"*Symptoms?*"

- "Heart skips beats and takes off to trot on its own
- stomach is jittery with butterflies

- knees weak
- no pain, but I want to scream."

"Diagnosis,
you are in love.
   Prognosis,
intermittent lifetime."

Potentially a First Date

"Isabel! Join me at the flower exhibition?"

"Sorry. I have to run. I have a date or two for lunch. Picked fresh yesterday off of a date palm tree."
(Phoenix dactylifera)

Reincarnation

Heather Hawk – I've been thinking about rebirth, after having had a conversation with people who believe in reincarnation.

I take my *second,* first breath. Then, my wail is heard throughout the maternity floor.

I hear crying behind me and see my limbs covered

in blood. I weep as well and howl. "This wasn't
supposed to happen! That witch doctor said the poison
was permanent."

Treasured

Shiny, gold sparkled rays. *What is that?*

Scraping away the desert sand, the transient sees a
jeweled heart embedded in a chunk of granite. The
transient digs further. Is it futile? He has scraped for
five hours. His eyes, absorbing the laser-like reflections
of the sun, have become cauterized.

Twins

Even before we were born, we've always been fought
over. Center of attention, center of heated disputes.
Mom wanted to name me Frances, Dad wanted Francis.

Fortuitously, they both got their way.

2   50 Word Shorts

Identity Crisis

Previously published in "50 Give or Take" Jessica Bell 2024
Heather Hawk – Inspired by a bumper sticker, which related
a truck to an electric car! !

"I want a Hummer!"

We haul heavy rocks driving off road into the desert. An ATV is the only vehicle that can handle the weight and the terrain.

"But what of the environment? Those vehicles use a lot of fuel. EV is best."

"No problem. I identify with a Prius."

Birth and Fate

There are things, Absyrtus my son, I'd like to express to you: the sound of birds' wings whispering through the air. Soft, blue-gray skies with towering cumulonimbus. Lightning. However, my emotional flames extend to Oedipus' hamartic fate. I'm the dusk, the opening, the essence, and the finality of your life.

The Last Thread

My husband's flannel pajamas are now a memory. Holes in the elbows, frayed neckline. Yet I've worn them to sleep for the past 10 years.

"I miss you, Babe."

His musky odor has faded from clothing, bed and pillows. One thread of memory remains.

I'll sleep with him no more.

Hoarding

Previously published in "50 Give or Take" Jessica Bell 2024

I collect books with different colored spines. Not to be read, but to decorate my walls in a geometric pattern.

Imagine the stories within revealing emotions of cool cerulean at the ceiling stacked over calm neutral sepias. Hot vibrant vermilions exploding on the floor. The room is made smaller, cozier.

Waiting for the Melt

Nineteen degrees. I'm very tired, shivering, sitting, and afraid to move on frozen Vermilion Lake in Canada. The sun begins to melt the snow. Soon, the thin layer of ice will melt, and I'll be with the fishes.

The water envelops me. Soft and soothing. I feel no pain. "A-h-h."

A Government Drone Surveilling a Global Movement

A thousand faces looking up tightly enveloped by trees. Although they move in unison, one will attempt a way out.

Loud speaker booms, "Lean left."

Crowd yells, "No, lean right."

I'm staying put in the middle.

"How dare you try something different! Move with us. We'll take a border down."

Imagine

I will not stare too long. Just a peek. I only need a glimpse for a flash fiction idea. My imagination will transform my neighbor's simple appearance.

Rob has morphed into a robin with his red face. Mary is slowly mutating into a poodle within her lamb's wool fur coat.

Inevitable

Previously published in "50 Give or Take"
2024 John McCaffrey

I dusted off the lint on the exterior of the dryer as well as off the gasket. The interiors of the dishwasher, refrigerator, and oven get a monthly thorough cleaning. The check-list of chores I rebelled at doing as a teenager, I am doing now. I have become my mother.

Self-Portrait
Previously published in "50 Give or Take"
2023 Elaina Battista-Parsons

Stranded on an island, I yearn without hope for rescue. Someone was here before. Their bones are left behind with a few personal belongings. I dare not touch them. Yet I use sand and my blood to draw my facial likeness in the sand. Might I be rescued today?

Disparity of Thanksgiving Festivities
Soft lighting for dinner. Family hugs and pets sniff in greeting.

"Turkey's cooking. One hour until dinner!"

A lone driver is forgotten after hours. Hugs his bottle, swerves. Power pole down.

Lights out. Family warms by fire. Dinner is cold.

Lights out. Driver's arms hug the wheel. Driver is cold.

The Sleep

Tuned for music, a conductor hears castanets clicking, a French horn's mellow sounds, and trembling vibrations of a bass clarinet all night long. The cacophony kept her awake for years.

She doesn't sleep and turns to face her husband. Her baton's slicing movement cuts the air. The "orchestra" is silenced.

Night Jogging

Previously published in "50 Give or Take"
2023 Elaina Battista-Parsons

As active as I was in the day, so I was in the night. I jumped into an active deep sleep, where my flailings woke my partner, but never me. Known sounds of traffic and airplanes were common and not a threat… I woke refreshed.

Midnight Snack

Winter camping in the snow. I wrap a blanket around me while roasting marshmallows in the fire. Breathing in the sweet vanilla caramel and dusty powdered sugar. Yum! I could eat a bagful.

Gasping for breath, I woke in my bedroom surprisingly satiated.

Heh! Where is my fluffy latex pillow?

Double Image

I don't recognize myself anymore. Trying to turn back the ages, I massage nighttime rejuvenation cream onto my face.

Come morning, we bound out of bed. Mr. Atlas admires his stance.

I look into the mirror reflecting an unfamiliar wrinkled face and:

"You are beautiful."

That's what the sign reads.

Cloud – Circa 1980

She writes in cursive. He types into a computer.

"I've heard that computers can get viruses. For safety, I'll put pen to paper during this cloud burst."

"Are you kidding? Anthropomorphizing a machine?"

"Yes, it sounds nuts. Next you'll hear that electro-magnetic storms can fry your document in the clouds."

Sentiment

As we are one little spark in this universe, so is one cell in our body. Cell changes are felt. Such it is in the cosmos. Picture an aquarium. A polyp in coral, that's us. What's the effect of a polyp's death on the aquarium? That's essence of the universe.

All Dressed Up and Nowhere to Go

Retirement's great. No conflicts, no commute. Freedom to sleep and play whenever I choose. Yet, I still have the mind-set to suit-up in professional attire and eat a standard breakfast. By habit, I reach for the car keys and head for the door. Then I realize, I've nowhere to go.

1970s Alternate Universe

Heather Hawk – Inspired by reading past travelogues.

The hotel advertises air-conditioning and music in every room.

Upon arrival we find the room has a fan and isn't refrigerated. No radio nor television. Music blares from the outdoor dining terrace.

Taxies are transport on four legs. A howdah.

Room service means fish from your window. Are they kidding?

Pure Model for Social Services

The crows' social behavior scouts for the needy.

We failed to attract small birds to the feeders. But the raucous caw-cawing of a single crow told of the seed. Within minutes, flocks of chickadees, sparrows, and juncos were feeding at their new home.

If only we could be so pure.

In Defense of Nature

Previously published in "50 Give or Take"
2024 John McCaffrey

Our garden is an overgrown jungle. Chaos abounds. An undefined garden with no definite paths to take, no sculpted areas. Vines invade wherever they please.

Barberries untamed thorny branches display like fireworks. My garden, like Earth, is beautifully unique.

My husband eyes the garden maliciously, "Get the machete, mower,…!"

"NEVER!"

3   *100 Word Epiphanies*

Poor Jacob

Daily at five p.m. I walk past 1st and Main. Poor Jacob stands on the northeast corner by a homeless shelter holding a cardboard sign with painted words: "No Food. Please Help" or "Hungry. Please One Dollar."

I gave one dollar each day, except once I passed him a coffee. We chatted for a few minutes. He smiled, "Thank you. Today marks my third full year on the corner."

Poor Jacob.

The next day, in a city park a block from 1st and Main, his body was found with his backpack on. Filled with 1,094 dollar bills.

The Glass Menagerie

*Heather Hawk-A writers' group prompt on the word 'glass'.
I wanted to write about reflections. My first thought was
Alice in Wonderland. Then I thought, could I write a story
using the word or a concept of the word from titles of songs
and movies? I played with quite a few titles.*

Cinderella dated the "Man in the Mirror," who has a
"Heart of Glass." They danced in his "Castle of Glass"
in a "Room Full of Mirrors." Her glass slipper was
broken and she died "Walking on Broken Glass."

Alone in her room, Maleficent hears a whisper. "Go
To The Mirror."

"Magic Mirror On the Wall-Who's the Fairest of
Them All?"

"I'll be Your Nightmare Mirror," replied the Mirror.

Is there transparency, *Through the Looking Glass*?

Look into "A Mirror of Deception." Then take a
"Whiskey Whiskey" to heal your broken heart.

Salud! Raise your whiskey glasses to Chihuly's
glass blowing.

Dreaming of a Dinosaur

My recently widowed ninety-year-old mother wanted to paint dinosaurs. To cheer her, we walked a jungled landscape where Jurassic Park was filmed on the island of Kauai.

"You won't find dinosaurs here," I informed her. "They were extinct millions of years ago. The largest reptile we'll see will be a lizard."

Said with determination and hope, "I'll paint a lizard!" She set up her easel.

Sighting movement, I exclaimed, "Wait! Look at that old codger with wrinkled, lizardly, sun-burned skin. I estimate he's about six-foot-two and comfortably bulgy, wearing plaid shorts from the 1940s era. Paint him. He's a dinosaur."

A Last Meal Nightmare

I've a bone to pick. And it's mine.

My solitary assignment to catalogue wildlife in the Mojave Desert was completed seven days ago, but tragically, without communication, my sponsors abandoned me. My crepey skin hangs on my skeleton as a curtain drapes over a rod.

Famished for that pigeon's wing bone, I'd torn it from a feline's jaws. Tasted like chicken.

Tonight I'll hunt with that feline.

Mohave cats hunted successfully and by morning I've lost many opportunities.

The sun burns my skin. Smells like barbecue. I wonder if my crispy skin will taste like chicken.

That is my nightmare.

Stasis

I heard voices in the distance. Passerbyers on the sidewalk?

Just waking, my eyes not yet open. I had had so many dreams, I wanted to relish a few more sleepy moments, but I'm hungry. Eye slowly flickers open. Still in that state of stasis between waking and dreaming, I couldn't yet move.

A woman dressed in a white cloak stands by my bedside. "You're awake!"

I try to answer, but no words come out of my parched mouth. My tongue sticks to the roof of my mouth.

"You're thirsty? That's understandable. You've been in a coma for three years."

"Wingmans" Diverted Flight Path

George aimed and grinned. Another paper airplane found his target. He was proud of his creations and their trajectory. He'd spent hours folding and flying different designs, each one surpassing the last.

His mother reprimanded, "Stop launching those planes inside!"

"I'm not breaking anything!" George protested. His face lit up, "I'm going to be a pilot, when I grow up."

"I know, but practice outside." Another plane floats by.

"Now!" she reprimands. "Outside. Dad will practice with you."

George's eyes sparkled. "He'll help me carry this two-foot model."

Mother hides smile. *"He'll join the Mile High Club when he's older."*

One Cutting Day in a Life

Heather Hawk - A writing groups 100-word prompt of 'Scissors'. Inspiration came from a boyish haircut when I was 12-years old and from falling asleep in the dentist's chair.

A drilling from a dentist is a more satisfying procedure than a styling from a hairdresser. The most comfortable recliner is a dentist's chair. The curves relax any tension and I doze.

During lunch, the resulting exquisite gold tooth, inlaid with diamonds, slices easily through my steak sandwich.

The upright hard hairdresser's chair faces the mirror into which I stare, agonizing over the jagged cuts. Is the length too long? Several additional sharp triangular cuts frame my square jawline. Now too short!

Outraged, I run to the gym and discharge a flurry of clipped scissor kicks at a life-sized dummy.

Boredom

Heather Hawk-This story was born from environmental disasters and some peoples' opinions.

"Oh, I'm just hanging here. I'd get a jump up but my flippers are too short. There's no current to propel me. Coral and seaweed? Gone. I'm suffocating. Where are the fish? Climate warming has changed all that. The larger fish either wash up on shore or swim north. Fishermen catch the smaller ones. It can take days before a meal comes my way. The water's murky. Sludge and debris flow into my habitat and it's hard to see thru the detritus. There's nothing here. I'm so depressed. How can I escape?"

Psychiatrist: "Eat chocolate! No charge for this session."

Nine Lives Are Not Just For Cats

Hours casting without a bite. Yet, I feel lucky on my third of nine lives. The surf is smooth! Soft breezes float against our backs.

Suddenly a tug - another struggle. The pole's

ripped out of my hands and taken out to sea.

He's furious. "Bitch!" Grabs my hair and pushes me under the water.

Holding my breath, *He's going to kill me!*

Struggle. No breath, limp.

"What have I done?" He jerks the back of my jacket up, "Get up you loser!"

Quick, CPR.

One quick breath, then another. I'm feeling lucky. Another life to live.

"Good riddance Charlie!"

Deep Dive Bar

Entering 'Fathoms Under the Sea', I graciously undulate to the bar and order my usual 'Ocean Mist' with blue curaçao, coconut, and vodka. There's time to change before tidal waves come in.

"Heh babe, can I buy you another?" A sharkish stranger nudges my shoulder.

The grouper bouncer gives the customer a piercing look.

A wrassey bus-boy, quickly squeezes in between us

as my tentacles begin to emerge.

I've slowly transformed. After spending more time scuba diving than walking on land, I identify and communicate with octopuses who gave me the means to evolve naturally.

Bus-boy loves my long arms.

Bondage – (a play date)

Heather Hawk – This story was written with a one word prompt 'bondage'. To show restraint I wanted to play with the concept and use one sentence with words in alphabetical order.

Rather than meeting in her apartment for their weekly tryst, Xanthippe (Alice) directs her playmate to a maximum security prison. Xanthippe chains Dalia in a fantastical cell bed. Dalia (George) begins her sing-song alphabetic requirement.

"Alice binds conversational dialogue every Friday. Forced George here, in jail. Kinky linked metal mail. Now, on purpose, quietly raising sword to umbilicus, very whirry. Xanthippe yells, " Zorro!"

Dalia, anticipating the extreme pain that Xanthippe could inflict, raises her chained arms to stop her lunging. "You can't keep me here! I cannot be bound in verbal bondage. **Fini**!"

Xanthippe unlocks the chains. Rapture ensues.

Cloud - circa 1994

Stormy weather, but cozy inside. She writes in cursive. He types into a computer.

"Between computer viruses and thousands of hacking incidents, aren't you afraid of your work being hi-jacked? For safety, I'm writing out this classified work."

"You'll be all afternoon. I can rip out double your content this afternoon."

"Besides no document access due to power outages, next you'll hear that electromagnetic storms can fry your document in the clouds."

"Don't cloud my mind with your nonsense. I suggest you write in the garden under jolts of lightning for inspiration. I predict a cloudburst will smudge your ink."

Riding on Silk

The discontented Prince of Rada needed a lighter than wool, more environmentally safe mode to travel over the Burafia Sea. He contacted his royal advisors who recommended a light weight fabric.

His subjects advised, "Our finest silk is much stronger and smoother, thus providing a more aerodynamic ride."

The Prince was ecstatic with his new transport. The threads, silky smooth texture shimmered in the sun. He boarded and the wind quickly brought his carpet and sail higher. The speed surpassed wool models.

His loyal subjects saluted as the Prince laughed and danced. Until the silk slipped out of his hands.

The Crush

Previously published in "100 X 100" Volume 2 2024, Manawaker Studio
Heather Hawk-Another word prompt 'Crush'. I wanted to use the word in several different contexts.

Harvest is complete and we are crushing grapes. My love gets juice on her lips and fingers as we gyrate to rock music to quicken the crush.

I crushed the sommelier's exam and will open a wine bar with Rose by my side. My heart soars with promises I will make to her.

My love's sultry look has an effect and I want to lick the splattered juice from her face.

"May Ralph and I get married in your vineyard this summer?" Rose asks coyly.

My heart is crushed as I squeeze the last bit of juice from thick-skinned grapes.

Eavesdropping-Who's Really the Nosey Neighbor?

Heather Hawk —Although the prompt was Eavesdropping, I'm in tune with houses and only thought of soffits and eaves. It took an altered voice before I was able to turn that viewpoint into listening.

The doorbell rings. I am loathe to answer because of frequent unsolicited door-to-door sales.

"Hello ma'am, I'm here to give you an estimate on your soffit and eave repair."

"I never requested an estimate. There isn't a problem with our roof." I slam the door shut.

"Who was that?" my daughter asks.

"A scammer trying to give an estimate for soffit and eave work."

"But, I called him after I overheard our neighbors stating that the eaves, dropping at the end of our roof, needed repair."

"Nosey neighbors! Can't mind their own business. And you! Why were you listening in?"

Decisions

There's a crumbling stone fence at the back of our property that's protected us from storms, wildlife, and sloughing of the steep land.

Our adjoining neighbor, Mr. Snodgras, wants to replace it. Says it's unsafe, not to code, and unsightly. My wife's ancestors built it in the 18th century. She had an unwavering strong sentimental attachment. Said she would rather die than replace one stone. She jumped last night.

While standing on the fence and surveying the land, I contemplate my options.

I'm conflicted on whether to replace the fence or join our ancestors and jump into the canyon below.

The Embrace of Pillows

So soft. I lay on pillows and rather than counting sheep I count imaginary pillowy white clouds against a blue sky.

As kids we tore pillows apart in exuberant combat. Pillows protected my knees from hard floors.

Of course, pillows are best for sleeping.

I bear hug one. Another squeezed between my legs cushions bones that once used pillows for exercise.

The soft satin cover feels slippery and cool against my face. As I sink deeper into the pillow it hardens as my face molds into the feather and foam.

97, 98, 99 clouds…drifting…while my caregiver calms my cancerous life.

The Case for Restricting AI Use to Grown-Ups

"We were arguing about the general populations' mental acuity. I referred to a study on how younger people are tuned into AI with computers handling their thinking processes. Using robots or virtual reality to handle their lives and activities, they are living in a fantasy world."

"I acquiesce. Using AI and virtual reality should be reserved for us gaming mavericks over 70."

"You're fantastical."

"Yes, I can be in my second childhood. There's no one to tell me what I can and can't do while acting as a child."

Her eyes pierce her husband.

"Except you, of course, my dear."

Secrets on the Lips

Heather Hawk — I had been thinking about today's tell-all books when a writers' group prompt suggested we write the true confessions of an inanimate object that had something to confess.

I wonder where we're going tonight. Today, she's put my sister's pink cream on. Probably shopping for clothing.

I'm a deep burgundy, she reserves for night outings and we're hot together. I'm a hard stick she applies to her pillowy hyaluronic filled lips. I love laying on her. She attends the most extravagant galas with celebrities. Oh, the places I've traveled, the celebrities I've kissed, and left my mark on! I could reveal over a hundred tabloid worthy scenarios.

But to reveal anything, she'd seal my fate. Leave me in the cosmetic drawer. Ultimately, my reveal remains on her lips.

Betrayal From a Dog's View

I love my mistress. I'll follow my mistress anywhere and stay by her side.

I've never seen that poodle before. Will my mistress feel betrayed if I sniff that poodle? She smells like freshly turned earth. Her fur is lovely and soft. Her wiggle is enticing. She feels so smooth and warm.

O-O-O-Whooof!

I've strayed loving a poodle. It's simply traitorous. I think I'm in love. I know I'm in love.

Oh dear, the poodle has run off and left me.

I love my mistress. Will she take me back? I'll follow my mistress anywhere and stay by her side.

4   Flash Fiction

Dumbfounded

Annette McCully - A movie received considerable fanfare on release, but I was flummoxed by its story line, costumes, and script. There seemed to be no point to the film.

I was dumbfounded as I left the theater. So this is what the critic meant when she skipped the plot description in her review. She said all she could think of after seeing the film was the female lead's face.

I could not find a way to express what I felt. The heroine was a blend of suicidal tendencies and infancy, with no real feelings for anyone, yet I felt cautiously sympathetic toward her. The poor thing lived in palace-like surroundings with turrets and crenellated towers. The floors were black and white squares, suitable for the throne room of the Queen of Hearts in *Alice in Wonderland*.

She had the company of genetically blended animals, like the dog with a duck's head, which was surreal but oddly normal. She wore richly colored clothes with stiff bodices and huge balloon sleeves and her hair was nondescript. The background was similarly drawn, the stuff of fantasy, with cartoonish curved walls and arched doorways.

The heroine was comedic and perpetually sexual but detached, indifferent to but yearning for her zealous lover. Alas, she has no message for us.

In Love with Whom? (Oreocereus celsianus)

Heather Hawk – Because of the hundreds of gardens I have toured.

Why do I consider the strange habits in others to be normal in my life?

Violet's bathroom overflows with plants. Plants on the window sill, counters, shelves, toilet tank, floor, in the bathtub, hanging from walls, shower rod… need I go on? Don't be surprised nor aghast. My predicament is similar. I'm addictively in love with 75 furry Old

Man of the Andes lining my windowsills. How long will the attraction last?

Clay Will Bind Us Together

Heather Hawk – This was inspired by a prompt about a couple returning from Spain. They could not leave a room until they came to an agreement.

Arriving in England from Spain, a customs officer detains a couple. "Spot check. Wait for an agent in that room, while we check your baggage."

Man, whispering to his wife, "It must be its heavy weight. I told you the package should have been mailed."

"I love this pottery. I didn't want to risk losing it. The designs match and complement our existing decor."

"But they are toxic. We can't eat off the plates; we can't touch the surfaces without damaging our cells. We have to solve this before the customs inspector returns. Either we keep it for show or we return ship it and let valuable goods out of our control."

"Either way it's a loss. Keeping it will ultimately be bad for our health. Returning it will be bad for our reputations."

"We both want the same thing for our future. Long healthy lives and successful business ventures together."

"So what do we do? I don't want to live without these mementos of our treks through the mountains where we used sand to seal the goods."

"We will return the dinnerware by mail, save for the serving platter that will look good above the doorway, and we'll keep the vases, *as intended*. At least we will receive partial reward payment."

Customs Officer Derek enters and states, "We have a recording of your conversation. A search of your baggage revealed your past itinerary to several private homes of key political candidates. The clay pottery will be confiscated as it was reported stolen. Come with us."

Wife whispers to husband, "I wonder if they know about the radioactivity and if they found the explosives?"

House Hunting

Heather Hawk

The Plumes are relocating from the high desert into the outskirts of a small town. They have just flown in and are anxious to set up house.

Mr. Plume has surveyed the area. "A large, single ground-level home may be available to occupy on Peacock Lane. We should take a look at it."

Without further hesitation, the couple arrives at their destination.

"Heh! What are you doing snooping in the windows?" the introverted Mr. Plume asks his new wife.

"I see no one," she squawks, while tapping on the window pane. Investigating further, tap, tap, tap. They walk around the corner of the glass-surrounded Arizona room. Tap, tap, tap. Still no response from inside.

The grounds are lovely. River rocks cover most of the sand, except there is soft compost and leaves under the bushes and trees which provide shade from the intense summer sun.

Mrs. Plume again taps a few times on a side window and peers in. They pause at the side gate admiring the landscape and peering in two windows. "This is so lovely, Hun. The kids will love the tree trunks and the low shrubs to hide behind. And the flowers on the orange tree are so scented to attract small insects."

Mr. Plume is a bit agitated as he struts along the exterior six-foot high cement block wall. "I don't know hun; this may be too expansive for us."

"Oh, don't get your feathers in a ruffle," she squawks.

"It is a safe compound though. Lots of open space for our babies to roam safely."

They continued bickering by chattering back and forth.

Mrs. Plume is satisfied. "I agree. Fully gated, no predators or robbers can enter. The fishhook thorns on the cacti and hidden thorns on the bougainvilleas are mean deterrents."

"Check out the ground under that Orange Jubilee. If acceptable, I'll gather the building material for our nest. This will be home."

All of this narrative played out as I observed the two quail through floor-to-ceiling windows from the interior of my home at 123 Peacock Lane.

Viewpoint Encased By Windows
Heather Hawk

A crisp sunny winter day reduces the depression that has overwhelmed Sarah over the past year. She was not yet out of the grief and adjustment stage of her restricted mobility.

After the accident, her father constructed a living room extension, and replaced the small two-by-four-foot windows with curved floor-to-ceiling windows. Outdoor scenes were seemingly brought inside and viewable from the kitchen and dining rooms. Sarah could sit for hours watching the town's activities, in this semi-circular area overlooking the city and the main boulevard below.

In the before time, she hated living on a noisy, busy street with the constant humming of vehicular engines and the occasional blast of horns. Now she was grateful for the activity. Parades during every holiday, street closures for festivals, seasonal bands, and occasional mimes entertained her. This was her private balcony.

It was just over a year since the accident. Sarah was an exuberant, athletic seventeen-year-old speed walking on the way to buy groceries when an icy softball-sized snowball sideswiped her head. The blow startled her so that she slipped and skidded downhill towards an oncoming Volkswagen. Her right leg could not be saved and a head injury damaged her cranial nerve resulting in bouts of dizziness and balance issues.

Today, she calmly sits and peers down at the children throwing snowballs on the green-way strip bordering the base of their property and running parallel to the boulevard. One of the older children pitches a snowball at the window. In a defensive move, Sarah tenses and ducks. As she hears the crack of the windowpane, she shrieks, and sees the resulting shimmering cracks. Her shoulders rise as she jerks her body sideways and her powerful arms begin to turn her wheelchair around quickly causing the chair to tilt on two side wheels. Her father hears Sarah whimpering and rushes in. "Sarah, Sarah! Are you all right? Here, I'll help you," and in righting the chair it thuds loudly on the wooden floors.

Closing her eyes, Sarah sighs and laments, "Please close the curtains. I never want to look through those windows again."

The Haunt
Previously published on Spillwords October 2023
Heather Hawk

The streets were lit by a clear starry sky and a nearly full moon. Four neighborhood children skipped door-to-door trick-or-treating.

Mary the Fairy led her friends; Fred the Ghost, Peter the Scarecrow, and Carla the Witch, along paths lined with lit jack o'lanterns, which was the tradition in the company small town where it was assumed that everyone knew everyone, except in the one dark Gothic-styled home.

The house was never lit. The uncovered windows reflected only darkness. No one ever crossed the door at 666 Portal Way, except during one late afternoon four years ago when the police escorted an old man inside.

It was rumored that a serial killer was sentenced to be imprisoned in the home. But no one really believed it, as the western town of Tombstone was one of the safest mining towns in Arizona, and the old man was never seen again after the police locked the convict inside.

As the four approached 666 Portal Way, the Fairy twinkled, the Ghost whooshed, the Scarecrow froze, and the Witch shrieked. The smell of fungi and overturned earth was pungent and putrid, yet sweet and so unrecognizable that Fred, Peter, and Carla gagged, wrinkled their noses and grimaced, "OOOUUU!" They turned to continue to the next home, except for Mary. Mary's curiosity was piqued.

"Y'all go on ahead. I'll get some treats from this house for all of us and meet you in five."

"But no one lives there," the Ghost foreshadowed.

The Witch advised, "Here, take this glass jar. It is filled with Himalayan salts, star bugs, and moon water. Should someone come to harm you, crack the jar and a protective shield will envelop you."

The Ghost, Scarecrow, and Witch wandered off to the next home to demand a Treat.

The Fairy in bare feet stealthily trod over moist algae along the north side of the house over the spongy fungi path. Heavy rains from the day before had not fully drained. This dampness was not typical in a desert town built on sand.

"Someone must have recently gardened." The smell of newly turned composted earth became stronger. "Someone must live here," she thought. "Perhaps occupying only the back of the house?" There were no jack-o-lanterns to guide her, so she lit her wand which sparkled and sizzled. The sizzle was the only sound and curiosity propelled her forward.

At 672 Portal Way, the residents were getting ready to leave for a Halloween costume party. Mrs. Krueger was dressed as an alien and Mr. Krueger wore street clothing and a life-like old hag face mask with fangs.

Ding Dong! The doorbell rang.

"I'll get it!" Mr. Krueger rang out as he strode to the door. He opened it and bent low to look into the faces of the Ghost, the Witch, and the Scarecrow who jumped back and screeched seeing his face and hearing his eerie laugh. What a Trick!

Mr. Krueger laughed again as he removed his mask and filled their bags full of candies. Mrs. Krueger came up behind him as he feigned a fearful surprise, with one arm and hand up he yelped, "Run before the alien points her magic ray gun at you and freezes you to this spot!"

The Scarecrow was so frightened he could barely move his sticks and had to be dragged to the next house by the fleeing Ghost.

Meanwhile, at 666 Portal Way, Mary's curiosity is further enticed by a smoky-sweet odor wafting from the back of the house. As she tip-toed into the backyard, a smooth tickle was felt around her ankle. She bent to look but was distracted by seeing apples on the ground. Looking up she saw the outline of what appeared to be a small orchard in the backyard. This

was atypical as all of the neighboring yards were xeri-
landscaped with cacti and succulents.

She heard whispering but could not make out all of
the words. "K—p stirring the -pples. - - bu— —g —-
sug-r."

The thought of a possible sweet caramel apple treat
was so irresistible she disregarded the feeling on her
ankles and focused on hurrying to the back door.

At the back stairs of the house, Mary turned to face
the porch and caught a glimpse of movement flowing
across the window. "Ahah," she thought, "indeed
someone does live here." Suddenly, from inside, a
figure turned to stare out of the window, looking
directly at the Fairy. The person had wide big eyes,
fangs for teeth, and grayish skin barely hanging on a
skeletal face.

The Fairy stiffened in place when again a smooth
tickle was felt around her ankles. She relit her fairy
wand looking down as gnarly long fingers encircled
her foot. No time to waste, she swatted the fingers with
her sizzling wand, burning them as they quickly
retreated into the algae and loose soil.

Freed from the grip, she ran out to the street to meet her friends who were a few houses away.

"Heh, guys! You will never believe what I saw. The house is haunted!"

"Yeah, wait till you hear this. Mr. Krueger is actually an old hag. He transformed right in front of us and his wife, De Vil, is an alien sorceress!"

And with this discovery of identities revealed, everyone in town now believed that they knew everyone.

The Mad Hatter Chef

Heather Hawk – Inspired by my husband's chef's hat, and my love of fashion. And, don't tell anyone, but we both have discussions with food.

The home chef was scurrying about the kitchen preparing for the evening meal at eight in the morning. They hadn't anticipated cooking indoors, but the Arizona wind was swirling around the house again, causing those pesky little dust devils. He wouldn't tolerate his starchy, white apron and toque blanche to become tainted by desert dust. Sir Basil Loin and Rosemary Sage were still adjusting to this new climate, having moved south from their vast estate in eastern Oregon last year to build their forever dream home. With year-round dry weather, they expected to host many outdoor dinner parties in their pergola-covered outdoor kitchen.

"Dang this inconvenient weather!" Basil slammed the dough on the granite island.

His still pasty-faced son ran into the kitchen, letting his stickball stick slide across the living room's tile floor. Beaming with a huge grin, Graham squealed, "You're putting together a dough batter!" and then pleadingly asked, "Can we have pizza tonight? Ple-e-e-a-a-se?"

"The dough will tell me. I've worked with this recipe before, and the pizza was thin and flexible. New York style. It will depend upon what the dough does in this no humidity, dry heat climate."

A near perfect indoor temperature of 92 degrees, the dough sits happily, alone to rise, in a small oven kept safe from drafts, accidental inspections from their cat, and unintended hits from their two clumsy boys playing stickball.

Hours later, Basil placed the bowl on the counter and looked at the rising dough. "What would you like to be today?"

"Bubble, bubble, burp!" The dough seems to be quite active.

"Calm down, Buddy. You weren't this happy in Oregon. It was all I could do to get you to rise there."

"Puuf, burp."

"Okay! Okay! You're going into the mother oven now!"

During the hour that it takes to bake the bread, Basil brings out the vegetables. "Carrots, you will be an accompaniment to string beans and roast beef. What is your preference for spice?"

The carrots are unusually quiet.

"Speak up or I will cut your manes off." The chef thinks his plump bunch of carrots seem to be happy by themselves. "String beans? What do you say?"

No response.

Basil becomes impatient. "I'll waterboard you!

Speak up!" Beans get swashed in a deep pan of water.

Beans squeak and squawk as their tips are being snipped. "No more, please! We'll take being sautéed in butter and crisp slivered almonds."

The carrots are not opening up. The chef snatches them up one by one and shaves their skin off. Slices every limb into half-inch pieces and sautés them in orange olive oil and an orange flavored brandy.

The oven bell rings and Basil checks the bread. A well-browned crust. He places the cast-iron pot on the stove top, and waits a few minutes to admire the bread. "Oh, you are beautiful, round and voluptuous. Just the right amount of golden tan." He turned the bread over and over in his hands, tapping all sides.

"Duh, duh, dudud," the bread responded to his taps, indicating that there are many air pockets under its crusty skin.

While allowing the bread to cool before slicing, he packaged and refrigerated the vegetables for a future dinner with his family.

Slicing the bread horizontally toward the bottom, Basil found a large air-pocket within the top portion.

He hollowed out more and removed his touche blanc. Trying the bread on for size, he discovered it fits perfectly on his head and the tan color softened his protruding bright carrot colored curly hair. A perfect topping for the ceremony tonight.

✝✝✝

The table was formally set for 10. Lace tablecloth, floral centerpiece, candles, water and wine glasses.

Invitations had gone out for an award celebration to recognize the best in fashion design. Guests were instructed to wear their self-designed hats and their latest fashion creation.

Basil had chosen a peony pink champagne with a blend of 55 percent pinot noir and 45 percent chardonnay. He opened the bottle, eliciting the soft pop and fizzle that is the Siren's prelude to his ears. He responded, "Good gracious! You are so tantalizing. A perfect perfume of fruit from the chardonnay and floral notes from the pinot. I love you." Allowing some of the effervescence to tingle on his cheeks, and then taking a splash to use as cologne on his neck.

Taking the first sip he heard the bubbles whisper, "My dance along your tongue will awaken your taste buds." Before he heard the customary champagne scream of "Take me!" the guests begin to arrive. Rosemary warmly greeted each guest with a crystal tulip-shaped glass, while Basil calmed himself and altered his disposition from his idiosyncratic talents to a froideur Master of Ceremonies. He greeted each guest as he expertly poured the bubbly.

Basil noted the predominant color scheme of each ensemble and assigned each guest a seat at the round dinner table in order of a color wheel. A fashion show ensued, directed by a now aloof Master of Ceremonies. After the modelers completed their walk and twirl around the room, Basil asked guests to be seated at the dining table.

Basil, not happy and dissatisfied with the color scheme, has the guests change seats to sit next to a guest dressed in a complementary color scheme. Satisfied, Basil announced his pick of the best hat. It wasn't just the deep red hue that caught his eye; it was the design that popped! O-o-oh-la-la! Russian netting in the shape of a thin disc was adorned with edible flowers in colors of a rainbow. Tassels of thin black pepper berries hung around the 16-inch diameter rim. Edible silver flakes dusted the entwined flowers, reflecting light, giving the appearance of dew.

His pick of the most creative ensemble was sea-themed. A suit covered in edible Irish moss. Cored apple slices served as buttons, long lapels were trimmed with vanilla beans, and oyster shells filled with oysters Rockefeller adorned the shoulders. A rare delicacy, which The Mad Hatter Chef craved, peeked out of the breast pocket - a small dried *te-nugu* anemone. A few grilled eel skins-*unagi*-hung from his trousers.

After cheers and accolades, everyone partook of a taste off of the clothing designs. In anticipatory delight, the guests were becoming hungry. "Bring on the food Basil! We've heard the way you prepare carrots is quite out of the ordinary." Another guest chimed in, "Perhaps wrapped in slivered scallops?"

The Mad Hatter Chef would never have guests chomp on his preciously prepared, delectable companions reserved for his family.

"I never mentioned there would be food, on the table."

The End of the World at a Kung Fu Temple
Raphael Pond - This story combines two of my favorite things: martial arts and the horrors of outer space.

On the first night, nearly all the stars in the universe disappeared. The only stars left in the sky were those of the Milky Way galaxy.

On the second night, all the stars in the Milky Way disappeared. The only celestial bodies left in the sky were the planets. During the day, the sun still shone, but at night, the sky was black and barren, except for seven lonely dots.

On the third night, the masters asked us to stay at the temple. Our temple sits on one end of a mountain ridge. At the other end of the ridge, there is an observatory where astronomers live. The masters said they were going to the astronomers to find out what happened to the stars.

On the fourth night, the masters returned. They looked troubled. We asked them what they learned from the astronomers. At first, they didn't answer. They said they needed time to meditate. Later that night, they gathered us in the courtyard and pointed to the black sky. The astronomers told them that space is expanding. It's ripping apart stars. It's ripping apart planets. It's pulling apart matter faster than gravity can bring it together.

On the fifth night, four planets disappeared – Uranus, Neptune, Saturn, and Jupiter. We saw them twinkle in the sky like stars. Then they dimmed and died within minutes. The astronomers told us that they saw it through their telescopes. They saw Jupiter stretch into a blob of loose gasses. The gasses further thinned until they vanished altogether.

On the sixth night, Mars and Mercury blinked out of existence. All that was left in the universe was the Earth, Venus, the sun, and the moon. Under the light of a nearly full moon, the masters gathered us in the courtyard. When I saw the face of a master, I saw something I had never seen before. Maybe fear. Maybe defiance. Maybe both. The masters told us that darkness was coming. This darkness could extinguish the light of the brightest warrior. We asked the masters if we should meditate. The masters shook their heads. Now is not the time to meditate. Now is the time to fight. The masters pointed to the sky. We must shine brighter than stars. The astronomers told us how stars work. At the center of stars, protons collide violently and let out huge amounts of energy. We will do the same, except more powerfully. We will collide our fists like protons. We will strike our knuckles together until they explode with energy – an energy that will defeat the darkness.

On the seventh night, we gathered in the courtyard. With our bodies, we made two circles – an inner circle that faced outward and an outer circle that faced inward. Every person in the inner circle had a partner on the outer circle. Even the masters joined the circles. They instructed us to punch each other's fists. We did as the masters said. We threw powerful punches at our partners and our partners threw powerful punches at us. Our knuckles clapped like thunder. One of the astronomers came down the ridge to our temple. He stuck his head over a wall and peeked into our courtyard. He looked very scared. Above him, a full moon hung in the sky. At the sides, the moon was breaking apart. Its luminous whole stretched and crumbled into dim bits. The mountain ridge became darker, almost pitch black – except for the Kung Fu warriors. Their fists collided repeatedly. With each collision, a shockwave went out, and the courtyard glowed with golden light. The warriors yelled with every strike. As they generated heat, their clothes caught fire. Above them, the fragments of the moon had thinned and disappeared. The darkness will be here soon. The astronomers say that the darkness is cold – colder than we can imagine.

My name is Yuze. I am 19 years old. I might be one of the last people left in the universe. I don't know if anyone will read this, but right now, I must go. My punching partner is looking for me. Together, we will join the circle. We will strike our fists to create energy. We will shine in the darkest of times.

A New Year's Forecast
Heather Hawk

An intense yearning of hope burned in Leticia's heart and soul as she lit a gas lantern, and placed it on the windowsill - the symbol that Leticia would still be waiting.

It has been four months since Eduardo disappeared. A year ago, they moved from the city to a forested area, after which he became depressed and often slipped away for weeks at a time on solo hikes into the hills, canyons, and open flat farmlands to alleviate his roller-coaster moods. Their log cabin on 30 acres was surrounded by a thick stand of old-growth conifers, and on occasion he felt the darkness to be oppressive from which he needed to free himself. Another of his meditative sojourns was rowing on Lake Samish with his wife Leticia.

Leticia was filled with memories of their picnic afternoons on the placid lake. She giggled slightly remembering one particular sunny afternoon. Eduardo had packed a heavy picnic basket and insisted on carrying it. "There are delicate accoutrements inside, not to be shaken." That particular statement engaged her curiosity. She couldn't resist and shook everything, trying to guess what each box held, while he prepared the rowboat.

Out on the lake, Eduardo opened the bottle of champagne which emitted a loud pop and a hiss. Whoosh! The force of the gases blew the cork 10 feet arcing out into the lake and a geyser foamed out of the bottle spraying droplets everywhere. Leticia had expected this. Giggling, she stood holding a fluted glass in her outstretched hand as she reached to catch the sun-sparkled waterfall. Her motion along with Eduardo's sudden movements shifted the balance of the boat, causing it to rock. Lake water reached the rail. They nearly fell overboard from the unexpected explosion and Leticia's belly-rolling laugh.

Over the months, there were many of these loving memories to keep her warm at night and anticipatory during the day.

The state had suffered a series of power outages over the past four years. Severe storms had downed power lines. Rivers overflowed, flooding many homes, and run-off caused landslides. Then, unusually severe cloud-to-ground lightning struck several homes, resulting in fire outbreaks. Looting, vandalism, and the breakdown of society followed. If you could safely reach an unpillaged store, supplies were limited or sold out. They no longer felt safe in the urban areas of King County.

It was time to move to a rural area and join his brother Juan, who had relocated to Whatcom County after a 10-year stint working in disaster relief. Eduardo and his brothers understood the importance of safety and following rules. Skills learned at an early age in the Boy Scouts were honed over the years. He had a 12-year career as a Navy SEAL and was an expert marksman and a proven survivalist.

The trio, Eduardo, Juan, and Jesús, were triplets with Eduardo and Jesús being identical. Jesús had settled in Jacksonville, North Carolina, to be near Camp Lejeune, where he previously trained as a Marine.

After a long discussion, with his wife, on the pros and cons of altering their lifestyle, Eduardo decided they would go off-grid. They found a log home located about two miles north of the southern boundary of Whatcom County and within five miles of his brother, Juan. A creek ran through the property near a small barn. There was a 150-foot deep well; a satellite dish would provide a connection to the news, and a generator to provide back-up power.

She had not regretted the move. Solitude, quiet, and the surrounding trees enveloped her like a cloak of invisibility. This fresh atmosphere was her solace, and she felt safe being alone in her sanctuary.

Leticia was a skilled homemaker and enjoyed cooking. She grew up on a small farm, and was not faint about dressing beef or cooking their raised poultry. The six chickens, two hogs, four ducks, and two goats kept her busy.

Recently, her primary contemplations and actions revolved around her husband's anticipated return. She stopped leaving the house to meet with friends, to not risk missing his arrival. Groceries and personal items were delivered. Cooking for one had not given her the same pleasure of preparing meals for loved ones. So she had continued to cook for two, and in her fastidious ways still dressed for dinner and placed her signature floral pins in her dark hair behind her right ear.

Television was her company. The news kept her up to date, and cooking shows provided enjoyment and new techniques to practice her creative culinary skills. Tonight she watched the news as meteorologists announced an unusual storm called a 'bomb cyclone'. Gaining in strength on its second day, the storm's easterly path was skirting counties to the south, and showing no signs of letting up. The howling wind and ice crystals pounded against the windows. Hearing thunder rattled Leticia's nerves. But she felt secure in knowing the generator would kick on should the power fail. Unfortunately, the gas lantern she had placed on the window ledge burned out and could not be relit. A sign? *No, it can't be,* she thought. Still having a deep belief that Eduardo will return, she thrust any negativity out of her mind and changed the channel to a cooking show.

The show featured a fish entrèe. Searching through the freezer, she decides to bake the lake trout that

Eduardo had helped her to reel in on one of their outings. From the refrigerator, she removes a crème brûlée batter.

For this evening's menu, she prepares a perfectly cooked crusted silver trout, steamed vegetables with hollandaise sauce, and a crème brûlée for dessert.

Setting the table for two with all dinnerware paired, including candles, she turns from the counter after pouring the last of a beautiful Sauternes. She gasps. *Is he really standing in the hallway? Yes!* He appears bedraggled with his hair uncombed and about two inches longer, almost reaching his broad shoulders. He is now sporting a beard and mustache. The new plaid jacket she had purchased for his birthday is stained with bird droppings on the shoulders and torn across his chest. One torn pant leg reveals a scabbed knee. Ignoring all this, she runs to him. She guides him to the table as he appears to be in a trance-like state.

"Here darling," as she hands the wine to him. "I have waited so long for your return."

"I've had a rough but enlightening commune with

nature these past few months," he said sipping the wine. "I would like to rest."

Leticia knew better than to ask. Eduardo was a man of few words. She would let him tell her in his own time. If at all. Those talks were reserved for Juan.

She spent the next day alone with him in bed before inviting her friends to join them for lunch.

Their best friends and in-laws, Juan and Sonya, feigned ecstasy about the news given over the phone. Juan was happy to hear from his sister-in-law but doubtful of her message. Typically, on Eduardo's return from retreats into the wilderness, the first person he contacted was Juan, and many tales and epiphanies followed. The twins always had a spiritual connection, which they exercised throughout their lives. They were taught the secrets of Santerías by their ancestors who all came from a long line of celebrated spiritualists.

During this last absence, Juan felt a broken or weak presence. At 35 years of age, there would be time ahead to correct and improve their spiritual bond. Perhaps Eduardo was testing a new ritual or spell and was purposefully blocking their connection.

Hearing a rumbling engine and then tires breaking the ice crystals on the dirt driveway, Leticia runs to the door to welcome her guests. "¡Date prisa! Entré. Eduardo está en la sala."

Juan and Sonya follow Leticia through the hallway. Entering the living room, they exchange questioning looks. They see no one.

Juan understands the transfer of spiritual connections between identical twins. He believes that Eduardo has placed their combined spiritual energy into comforting Leticia. Conceivably, Eduardo has already messaged Jesús who had always loved Leticia.

The crisis management plan was simple. Tonight he would begin a music ritual to invoke the dual deity Ibeji-the twins of the Orishas and guardians of the dead. Through Ibeji, he would receive messages.

He would place gifts in the creek for Oshun the Goddess of Love and rivers, who was the protector of marriage. He'd ask for guidance in communicating to Jesús the importance of being with Leticia and to take the next plane out.

This would be a new beginning for his brother and sister-in-law in the new year. After Jesús arrives tomorrow, he would take 'Eduardo' for a walk and return with Jesús.

Annie's Eyes

Eric Stathers - This is a story anchored on ground that was not well understood and purposefully concealed from public scrutiny sixty years ago.

It was always green. No matter the time of year, it was always green. Summer found it maybe greenish brown and in winter it was brownish green, but still green. Sometimes little riffles of wind danced along the surface, but the quiet depths moved slowly. Only the long stems and leaves of the grasses and plants along the edges gave away the secrets of its movement. Quick flashes of the sticklebacks or salmon fry as they raced from cover to cover were the only other movement. The only sounds were from the drops of rain falling from the over-hanging branches, the rustle of the wind or the rude splash of the kingfisher as he dove to catch the elusive salmon fry or sticklebacks. All this was changed where the drainage ditch behind the dyke was cleared and widened. Here the multi-colored fruits of our labors were stored in low rows. The carefully split cuttings from the roots of the willows, the red and yellow cedars and spruces and wild cherry were tied in loose bundles and held below the surface of the green water by long flat river rocks. When you looked at them there was little told of the hours of digging, pulling, splitting, and trimming of each piece. Nothing showed of the happy hours when the two young boys followed the stooped figure of their grandmother who was so intent on gaining this treasure. The boys were there for the fun of the day in the forest and to share in the goodies that Annie kept in the flour sack tied over her shoulder. There was a special basket that held a thick paste of meat or fish and another of berry jelly or jam that we ate with our bread followed by a sweet chewy candy. We ate the peeled stalks of the young blackberry canes or salmonberry bushes and then we went back to our game of getting the longest root. At the end of our day

Annie would coil the roots for us to carry over our shoulders. We went back along the riverbank to the one room shack on the log float tied on the outer side of the dyke where Alvie and Annie lived. So, the summer of my fifth year passed. I was a happy boy running free with my new friend Alvie, focusing on the immediate and not aware of the lore that I was exposed to.

Labour Day weekend came with much excitement as my father told me he had permission to send me to school to start Grade One. So, there I was with my new pencils and eraser tucked in my pencil box and my ruler tucked inside of my new red covered scribblers with a clean handkerchief in my pocket. I had it all. The shock came when I realized that Alvie was not there. He was almost a year older than I so he should have been there. No Alvie…no friends. The other kids from Sunday school were there, David, Bryce, James and even the girls, Iona, Violet, Patricia, and Tessie but not Alvie. I did not understand, and my mother could not tell me, as she did not talk to "clouches". It was the slang racist word used back then for Native women particularly those threadbare, weather worn older women that lived along the dikes or in the abandoned float shacks by the river. But to me Annie was my friend and guardian during those summer months. She and my mother were miles apart socially. Annie accepted all the brown paper bags of old dresses, shirts, and socks that I carried to her without a word but never a word would she speak to my mother. The mystery deepened. The world was a strange place to a five -and a-half-year-old.

Life carried on but, in my case, it was unfolding as it would.

By the age of sixteen I had much of the experiences and adversities that life has to offer. I was working as a contractor booming logs. Part of the job was to sort out the second-grade logs and move them up the river channel to the sawmill where they were to be processed. To my surprise and joy this one day who should be there to accept delivery of my logs, but my childhood friend Alvie. I greeted him with great enthusiasm but to my amazement he repelled my greeting with a nodded recognition. When pressed

into conversation he responded with minimal words
and no explanations as to where he had been and
nothing about his life since he had left ten years ago. I
went out of my way several times after that to eat my
lunch with him or talk to him every time we went to
town. Alvie remained silent. I could tell that he wanted
to see me and find a way to renew our friendship but
each time we met a curtain dropped between us when
we started to talk. I knew he was hurting inside but I
could not reach him. Summer went, and the rains of
October arrived. I was busier than ever trying to get
my work done and apply for school correspondence
courses, so I did not have time to search out Alvie and
talk. One day as my work partner and I stood out of
the rain under the roof of the boom winch, Kelly
casually said too bad about that Williams kid. An icy
wind went through my gut. What Williams kid? You
know… Alvie Andrews nephew…hung himself…they
found him hanging from the rafters in the woodshed
this morning.

It was dark at four in the afternoon when I left
work. Raining steadily as I rode my bicycle the three

miles on the rutted gravel road to the Andrews' home.

No sign of life was evident as I came up to the house. I leaned my bicycle against the rickety picket fence and went into the yard. I was apprehensive and did not know what to say but I had to go. At the corner of the house, I caught the sound of a quiet steady rhythm of a drum. Then I peered into the dark interior of the woodshed. When I got closer, I saw the worn soles of a pair of heavy boots. The body lay on two planks on sawhorses, the rope still around the neck. There was no mistake…it was my friend Alvie. The sound of the drum was now accompanied by a low keening sound and came from the darkness of the shed. I went in further and saw a hunched figure covered in a grey blanket crouched in the corner. The figure moved and a face turned toward me. It was Annie. Her thin grey hair hung about her face in unkempt strands. The top of her dress was wet from crying. She lifted her head to see me better and I looked into the deepest blackest eyes I had ever seen. There were no tears now…just the streaks on her face to mark their path and only a little life seemed to remain in the darkest recess of those eyes. She greeted me in her Salish tongue then said, "God Damn that residential school". Those eyes are embedded in my memory till today.

The End of Nancy Drew

Julia A. Hunter- "The End of Nancy Drew" originated as an entry for the Puget Sound Sisters in Crime's annual flash fiction meeting. The original story had to use Nancy Drew as its inspiration, keep within a strict 250-word limit, and contain five mandatory words. What started out as an obituary for Nancy Drew has changed format, doubled in size, and may or may not contain those five words.

I stopped typing and ran my eyes back up the screen, proofreading my latest update on the most sensational Beantown murder in this decade:

Multiple Persons of Interest in Death of Famous P.I., Nancy Drew

Boston's finest continue to probe the mysterious death of Nancy Drew, who was found dead at her desk in the Boylston Street, offices of Drew & Nickerson,

Private Investigators, on November 7 of this year. She was not alone at the time of death; someone pulled the trigger on the gun that shot her from several yards away.

Police are grappling with a large pool of suspects, the result of her many years as a private investigator. As her office manager, Bess Martin, said last week, "From her first case as a privileged teenager, Nancy questioned, pried, spied, researched, manipulated, and blundered her way to solutions, whether she was unraveling secrets in old clocks, chasing bad guys at mundane locations, or trolling through diaries, letters, and other documents to uncover dark truths. To be her friend was to be her assistant."

In addition to fifty years of successful and sometimes sensational detective work, Drew & Nickerson had recently undertaken several cases involving diamonds, murder, and political scandals, all of which remain active in the company's books. These add to the list of potential suspects.

Drew was personally in charge of all of the firm's investigations. Her closest relationships were with her colleagues, all of whom had been her friends since their teen years. At the time of her death, she and Ned Nickerson were still business partners, having recently divorced each other for the fifth time. When interviewed by "Good Morning, Boston!" during last year's adjudication, Drew stated, "I have no children except my cases; those are all I want keeping me up at night. I make no claim to any of Mr. Nickerson's offspring."

Nickerson will now step up to close the pending cases, with the help of life-long friends and employees Bess Martin and George Fayne. The small staff mourn Drew's passing. Fayne says that they feel "rudderless without Nancy's sense of direction and drive."

"Our top priority will be the discovery of the perp who killed our Nancy," Nickerson said at a brief press conference yesterday. "We will be cooperating fully with the Boston Police's Homicide Division even while we conduct our own, private inquiries."

As my finger moved toward "Send," I heard my name.

"Hey, Jackie! You're working on the Drew thing, right? Check out what just happened. BPD just announced they've brought in three persons of interest."

A Woof in the Dark

Julie A. Hunter - "A Woof in the Dark" originated as an entry for the Puget Sound Sisters in Crime's annual flash fiction meeting. The stories had strict 250-word limits, a crime-centered theme, and five mandatory words. The words were brolly, putid (which means pretty much the same as the more common "putrid"), dogged, persuasion, and synchronicity. The story has been slightly altered from the original as read at the event.

I leash the little beagle and grab my brolly. Wesley is the most determined canine I have ever known. He is absolutely dogged in his pursuit of all things putid.

Stepping out my front door into the thickly dripping fog, I fumble raising the brolly. Wesley takes advantage, yanking his leash out of my hand. He's off! — racing across the dark street and into our neighborhood park. Great. Tonight I can barely see the entrance from forty feet away.

I hear him yapping in his form of persuasion. Does he want me to join him, or has he found another loose dog, or…? Finding another dog loose would be notable synchronicity in our quiet street of row houses.

Using my phone's flashlight I pick my way across the street and follow Wesley's yap into the park. Much as I enjoy this cool, green sanctuary on a sunny day, I would not have brought us here tonight. Wesley's barks are louder, hysterical. He's beyond the first turn in the main path, and he's not alone when I get there.

A man is stretched across the path, face down. A closer look with my flashlight reveals a six-inch gash in his side with a big pool of blood spreading out.

"Damn it, Wesley, why can't you ever go off duty?" I demand. Then I check for the pulse that I know won't be there.

Hitting speed dial, I call my office. "Harry, I need a full incident team in Casey Park. Cadaver dog Wesley finds victims even on his evening potty walk."

What A Boy Needs

*Adapted from and previously published in
Brushfire Literary Arts Journal.*
Tracy Mears

He loved her. His copper-colored '66 Continental was the coolest car. A surprise gift from his father eight years ago.

There was no way to renew his car's tags after his poor girl failed emissions because of a cracked cylinder head. The county's test numbers on the paper readout had been so close, he decided to drive down to the DMV and see if he could get a waiver.

There, a tight-lipped woman with a ratty head of dyed hair handed him a number and nodded toward the waiting area. His head snapped to look at someone passing by. Graying crew cut, sweater vest, black-rimmed glasses. For a moment he felt a fleeting sense of recognition, but then it was gone. They had not spoken in six years, but still he imagined seeing his father.

Finally, he was called to the window. The bitter bureaucrat said he would have to spend at least $300 to repair his car before the state would grant him an emissions waiver so he could renew the registration. He tried to explain to the woman that he had no way to earn the money for repairs unless he could drive the car to work. "Next," she called out to the crowd.

All the way home, he prayed no patrol car would notice his expired plate. He parked the Continental in front of his studio apartment, then walked ten blocks to a sprawling corporate auto parts store. Inside, he had the uniformed employee with black fingertips look up the part number he needed. After a few minutes, the clerk returned and dropped the weighty, shiny new head assembly onto the scarred countertop.

With $33 in his wallet and the new head priced at $227, he hefted the heavy heads into his arms as if he were carrying a child.

He looked all around and then he ran and ran and ran.

THE END

We truly hope that you have enjoyed these stories. If they have inspired you in any way, please let readers know by leaving a review on social media pages such as Amazon, Goodreads or LinkdIn. Your review helps readers, and your feedback helps us as authors.

We welcome the opportunity to connect and discuss our projects.

- www.heatherhawk.net
- https://www.linkedin.com/in/heather-hawk-0774062b2/

Meet our Storytellers

Heather Hawk

After a career of writing factual reports in the real estate industry Heather transitioned to writing creative nonfiction, contributing to an anthology *"Tales From A Writers' Circle"*, and then self-published *"Running With Knives."* Newly expanded stories from that book with updated experiences are in an "Epi-blogue." Come visit at www.heatherhawk.net

Look for her short story "Long Enough" in "The Day that Changed Everything". December 2025, published by Brightspring books.

She now lives in flash fiction. Connect with Heather at https://www.linkedin.com/in/heather-hawk-0774062b2/

Julia A. Hunter

Julia Hunter is a historian by training and has published biographies of New England women; Anna May Sevigny, Cornelia "Fly Rod" Thurza Crosby, and Harriet Blaine. She has also edited newsletters and quarterlies. Since relocating from Maine to the Seattle area, she has retired from a museum career and become a suburban housewife who divides her writing time between family memoirs and fiction. She is the secretary of the Puget Sound Chapter of Sisters in Crime; this is a natural outgrowth of her deep love of mystery and detective fiction. She draws on her background as an editor when serving as a beta reader for some of her favorite authors.

Annette McCully

Annette Dennis McCully is the author of several handbooks on international standards, and was an aerospace technical writer. She has also been a poet in schools and libraries, a journalist to two international presses, and a consultant for proposals and corporate documents. She is currently working on her sixth book and writing essays. Her writing profile can be found at www.annettemccully.com

Raphael Pond

Raphael earned a degree in Professional Writing at York College of Pennsylvania. Most of his writing is hard sci-fi, magical realism, or both.

His debut novel *Bell Tower* was released in 2025. You can view his work at www.raphaelpond.com

Tracy Mears

Tracy Mears has won numerous awards for both fiction and nonfiction, including an honorable mention from PEN Women. Her work has appeared in Painted Cave and The Gila River Review. Tracy's piece "Home Sweet Home" reflects on her time with a traveling carnival, which was published by Swamp Ape Review.

You can read more of her work at https://tracymears .wordpress.com

Eric Stathers

Eric Stathers is the author and publisher of ten self-published books. He is retired and serves as a Board Member of the Lillooet District Historical Society. Eric graduated with honors from the University of British Columbia with an MBA and BSc in Agriculture, and is a graduate of the Stanford University Executive Management Program. Before moving to the United States, Eric worked in Canada in the mining industry and environmental consulting.

Works by Author

Heather Hawk
    In Love With Whom
    Clay Will Bind Us Together
    House Hunting
    Viewpoint Encased By Windows
    The Haunt
    The Mad Hatter Chef
    A New Year's Forecast
Julia Hunter
    Nancy Drew Obit
    A Woof in the Dark
Annette McCully
    Dumbfounded
Tracy Mears
    What a Boy Needs
Raphael Pond
    The End of the World
Eric Stathers
    Annies Eyes